Caillou

Plays Hockey

Adaptation from the animated series: Anne Paradis
Illustrations taken from the animated series and adapted by Mario Allard

It was a beautiful winter day. Caillou and his family were having fun at the rink.
Caillou loved to skate really fast.
"Wow, you're as fast as a rocket!" Daddy said.
Caillou was proud of being such a good skater now.

Some bigger kids got onto the ice.
Billy said, "Hi, Caillou."
Caillou loved to watch Billy and his
friends play hockey. They skated so fast!
"Daddy, can I play hockey with Billy?"
Caillou asked. "I'm a good skater.
I'm as fast as a rocket!"
"Let's ask Billy," Daddy answered.

Caillou felt shy. He asked Billy, "Can I play hockey with you and your friends?"
"Sure," Billy said. "Bring your gear and you can play with us whenever you like."
Caillou was thrilled.

Daddy took Caillou to a sporting goods store to buy what he needed to play hockey.
"Here's the secondhand equipment. When kids get too big for their gear, they trade it in here for larger sizes."
First Caillou tried on helmets.
"This one's perfect," Daddy said.

Daddy and Caillou chose gloves,
a puck and a stick.
"This stick's much too long for me,"
Caillou laughed.
The store clerk cut it to just the right
length. Now Caillou had everything
he needed to play hockey with Billy
and his friends.

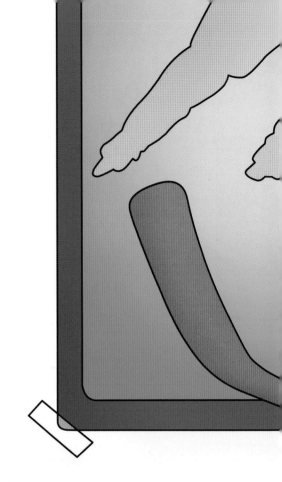

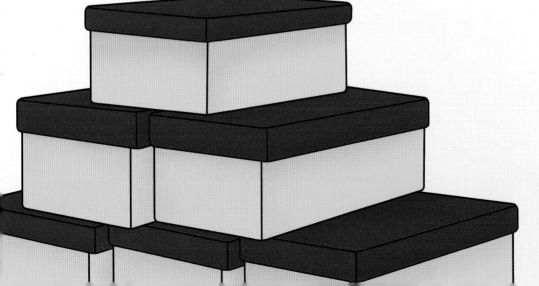

The next day, Daddy helped Caillou practice shooting
the puck. Caillou took a swing and shot the puck
straight at the goal.
"What a great shot, sport!"
Then Caillou stickhandled the puck down the ice.
He wound up and shot the puck right into the net.
Caillou jumped with excitement. He felt ready
to play with the big kids.

Caillou went to the rink that afternoon.
Daddy reminded him, "Playing hockey isn't as easy
as it looks."
The big kids were happy to see Caillou. Billy passed
the puck to him, but he missed it.

Caillou tried to keep up, but the game was much too fast for him.
Daddy was right: it was harder than Caillou thought it would be.
Caillou didn't feel like playing anymore.

"I thought you played pretty well," Daddy said. "Look, I've got something for you."

Daddy gave Caillou a hockey jersey. He tried it on. It was a bit too big, but he loved it.

"This was mine when I was young, Caillou. Keep practicing, and by the time it fits you, I bet you'll be able to play as well as Billy and his friends."

Daddy took Caillou to his friend Leo's house.
Leo had his very own backyard rink. Caillou was
glad to be practicing with his best friend. He knew
they would get better together.
"Here, pass me the puck!"
The boys worked on their passing.

Caillou and Leo pretended that they were playing in a professional league.
They were so good that they had no trouble getting the puck past the other team.
Caillou sped down the ice and passed the puck to Leo. Leo shot and scored!
The goal light went on, and the crowd went wild!
Caillou gave Leo a big high five.

That night Caillou was tired from his hockey practice.
But he was also very happy. He knew that someday, when he was big enough to wear Daddy's jersey, he'd be a really good hockey player.

Text: adaptation by Anne Paradis of the animated series CAILLOU,
produced by DHX Media Inc.
All rights reserved.
Traduction: Joann Egar
Original Episode #306: Caillou Shoots! He Scores!
Illustrations: Mario Allard, based on the animated series CAILLOU
Coloration: Eric Lehouillier

The PBS KIDS logo is a registered mark of PBS and is used with permission.

Chouette Publishing would like to thank the Government of Canada and SODEC
for their financial support.

Books
Tax Credit

Gestion
SODEC

Bibliothèque et Archives nationales du Québec and Library and Archives
Canada cataloguing in publication

Paradis, Anne, 1972-
[Caillou joue au hockey. English]
Caillou plays hockey
(Clubhouse)
Translation of: Caillou joue au hockey.
For children aged 2 to 6.

ISBN 978-2-89718-407-0

1. Caillou (Fictitious character) - Juvenile literature. 2. Hockey - Juvenile
literature. 3. Persistence - Juvenile literature. I. Allard, Mario, 1969-   .
II. Title. III. Title: Caillou joue au hockey. English. IV. Series: Clubhouse.

GV847.25.P3713 2017   j796.962   C2016-942542-8

Printed in China
10 9 8 7 6 5 4 3 2 1   CHO2004 MAY2017